MW00892950

Harcourt, Inc.

San Diego New York London

Printed in Singapore

Written by
Ann Braybrooks

PLENTY OF POCKETS

Illustrated by
Scott Menchin

Henry and Henrietta Bunch lived in a pocket of land between three hills. They lived

in a tiny house with their son, Junior, and a pygmy hedgehog named Max… and lots and lots and lots of stuff.

Junior's artwork crowded the walls. Henry's sculptures weighed down the couch. Henrietta's books rose from the floor in tall, tilting towers. Every inch of space was filled with toys and games and pots and pans and hangers and clothes and newspapers and magazines. Even the ceiling was cluttered with looping lamps and hanging plants.

One day, Henry could not find a toothbrush. Or a comb. Or his overalls. Worse, Henrietta coul

(which she had hidden). "We need pockets," said Henry. "Do you

not find Max, Junior, or Junior's birthday present

mean closets, dear?" asked Henrietta. "No," replied Henry. "Pockets."

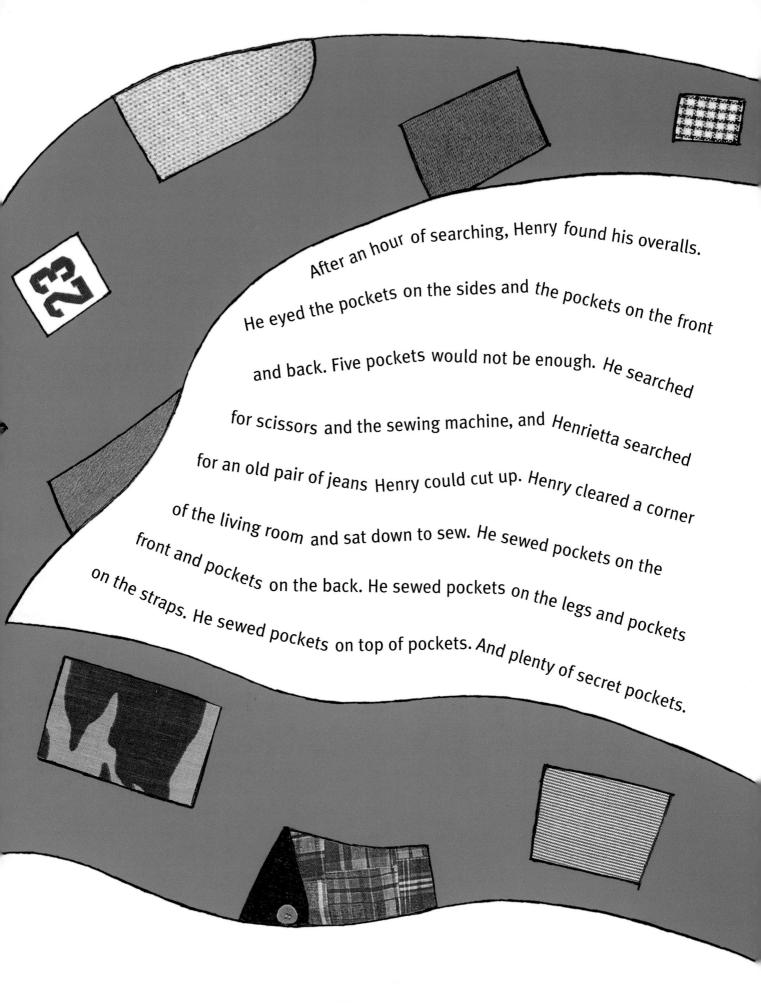

After an hour of searching, Henry found his overalls. He eyed the pockets on the sides and the pockets on the front and back. Five pockets would not be enough. He searched for scissors and the sewing machine, and Henrietta searched for an old pair of jeans Henry could cut up. Henry cleared a corner of the living room and sat down to sew. He sewed pockets on the front and pockets on the back. He sewed pockets on the legs and pockets on the straps. He sewed pockets on top of pockets. And plenty of secret pockets.

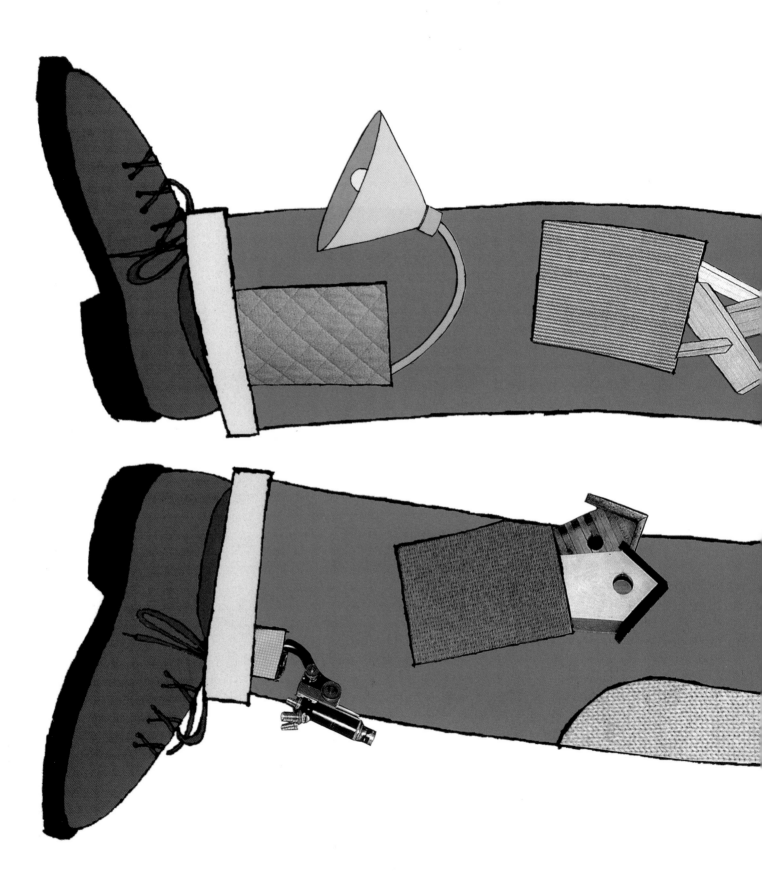

While Henry sewed, Henrietta found Junior and Max. As soon as Henry pulled on his overalls, she put Junior in a pocket on the front. She put Max in a pocket on top of Junior's pocket.

Then Henry and Henrietta filled the rest of the pockets in his overalls. In went toys and games and pots and pans, and forks and spoons and cups and plates. In went tables and chairs and books and bookcases. In went Junior's birthday present, which—thank goodness—they'd found in the bottom of a laundry basket. When Henry's pockets were full, Henry asked Henrietta, "Wouldn't you like pockets, too?"

She sewed her favorite dress, and Henry began to sew. He sewed pockets on the seams and pockets on the back. He sewed pockets on the seams and pockets on the front and pockets. And plenty of secret pockets. In went pockets on the top of pockets, until all that remained was Junior's artwork. "Like a museum!" said Henry, trying to keep the rest of the stuff, wobbling a bit. "Like a museum!" said Henrietta, "perhaps we should invite some neighbors over for Junior's birthday next weekend."

"I would," said Henrietta. She found her balance.

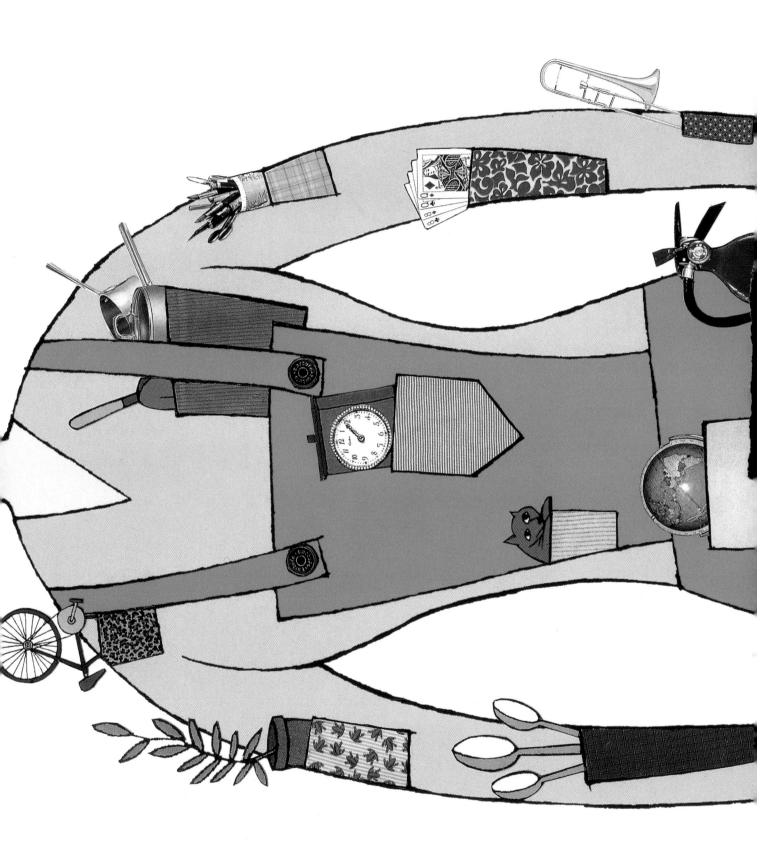

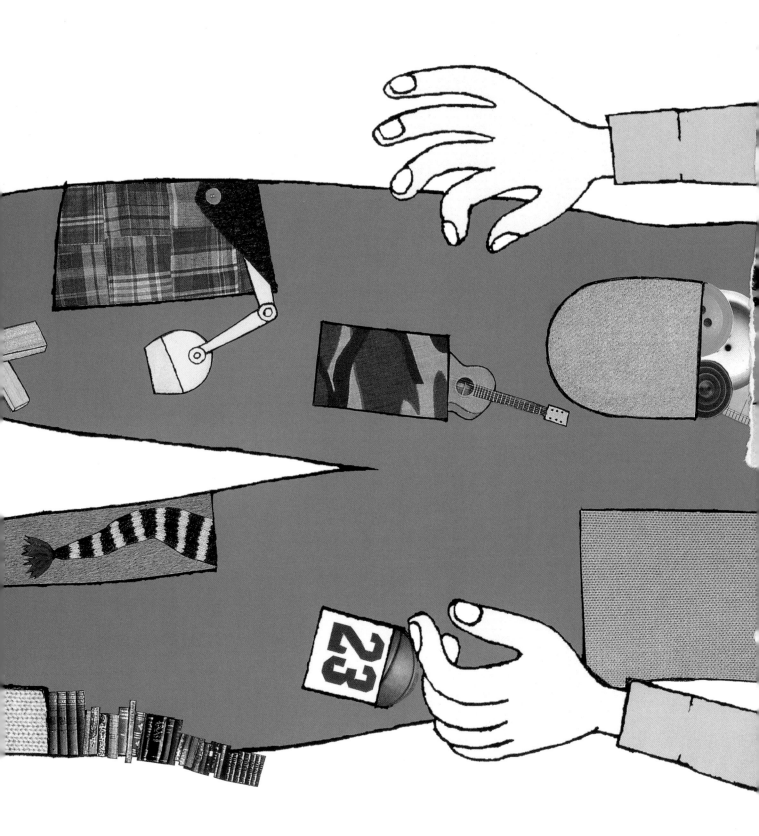

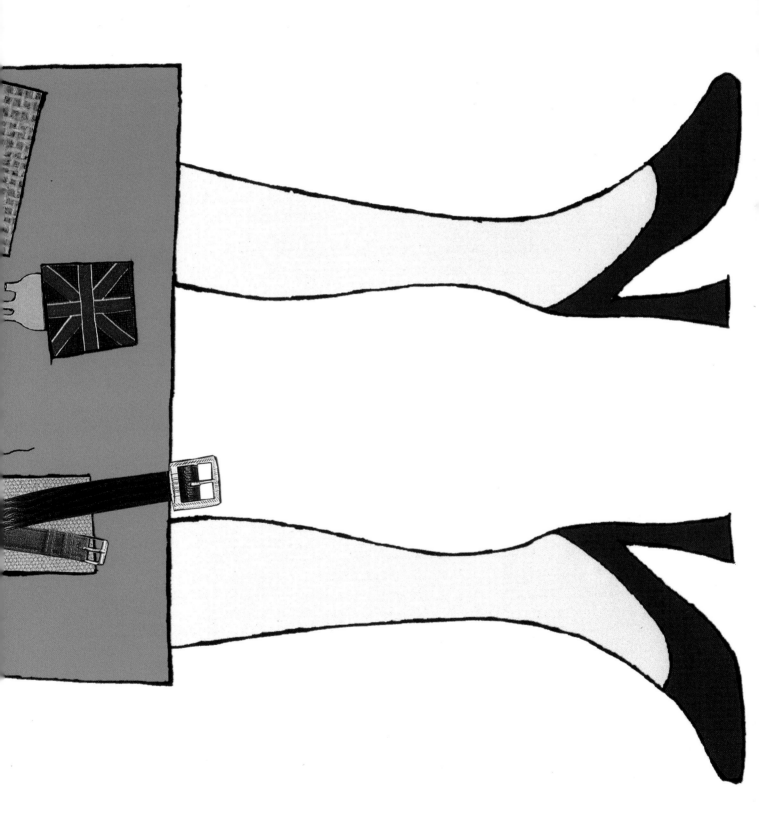

Henry stepped toward the door. Henrietta stopped him. "Henry," she said, "where will people sit? I put the sofa in one of your pockets." "Which pocket?" said Henry. Henrietta peeked in one pocket, then another, and another. She could not find the sofa anywhere. "I guess we'll just have to empty our pockets," said Henry, who was eager to see all of his stuff again. First Henrietta took Junior and Max out of their special pockets. When she saw how happy they were to roam and explore, she gently touched Henry on the arm. "Wait, Honey Bunch," said Henrietta. "Why don't we take Junior and Max outside, and empty our pockets there? We'll all have more room." Henry agreed. He carried Junior outside, while Henrietta carefully carried Max. Then Henry and Henrietta unpacked their pockets. Out came tables and chairs and books and bookcases. Out came forks and spoons and cups and plates, and pots and pans and toys and games. And, of course, the sofa.

Max and Junior climbed over and under, in and out, the tunnels and hills of stuff. As Henry and Henrietta filled the yard, the neighbors came by to watch. One offered to buy a chair. Another begged to buy Henrietta's collection of baskets. Henrietta sold the chair, but not the baskets. She put tags on all the things she didn't want, and the neighbors poured out of the hills for the sale. "Such delightful people," said Henrietta after the last neighbor had gone home. "So kind and generous!" said Henry, who had received ten orders for clothes with lots of pockets.

That afternoon, Henry and Henrietta carried all of their favorite stuff into the house. Junior and Max helped. For a few days, Henry and Henrietta kept their house tidy, with everything in its place. Henry wore his overalls, and Henrietta wore her dress, with only a few things tucked into the pockets. All was neat and clean, until...

Junior ha

Happy birthday

To my honeyBunch, Paul
—A. B.

To Masha and Ivetta
—S. M.

REQUESTS FOR PERMISSION TO MAKE COPIES OF ANY PART OF THE WORK SHOULD BE
MAILED TO: PERMISSIONS DEPARTMENT, HARCOURT, INC.,
6277 SEA HARBOR DRIVE, ORLANDO, FLORIDA 32887-6777.

LIBRARY OF CONGRESS CATALOGING-IN-PUBLICATION DATA
BRAYBROOKS, ANN.
PLENTY OF POCKETS/ANN BRAYBROOKS;
ILLUSTRATED BY SCOTT MENCHIN.
P. CM.
SUMMARY: HENRY TRIES TO SOLVE THE PROBLEM OF HIS FAMILY'S MESSY,
CROWDED HOUSE BY MAKING LOTS OF POCKETS AND PUTTING EVERYTHING
AWAY IN THEM, BUT THE SOLUTION IS NOT A PERMANENT ONE.
[1. ORDERLINESS—FICTION. 2. POCKETS—FICTION.] I. MENCHIN, SCOTT, ILL. II. TITLE.
PZ7.B73884Pl 2000
[E]—DC21   98-53784
ISBN 0-15-202173-6

FIRST EDITION
A C E F D B

THANKS TO MASHA FREYVERT AND TAYLOR SHUNG FOR CREATING JUNIOR'S ARTWORK

THE ILLUSTRATIONS IN THIS BOOK WERE CREATED WITH PEN AND INK AND COLLAGE.
THE DISPLAY AND TEXT TYPE WERE SET IN METAPLUS BOOK.
COLOR SEPARATIONS BY UNITED GRAPHIC PTE. LTD., SINGAPORE
PRINTED AND BOUND BY TIEN WAH PRESS, SINGAPORE
THIS BOOK WAS PRINTED ON TOTALLY CHLORINE-FREE NYMOLLA MATTE ART PAPER.
PRODUCTION SUPERVISION BY STANLEY REDFERN AND GINGER BOYER

DESIGNED BY IVETTA FEDOROVA

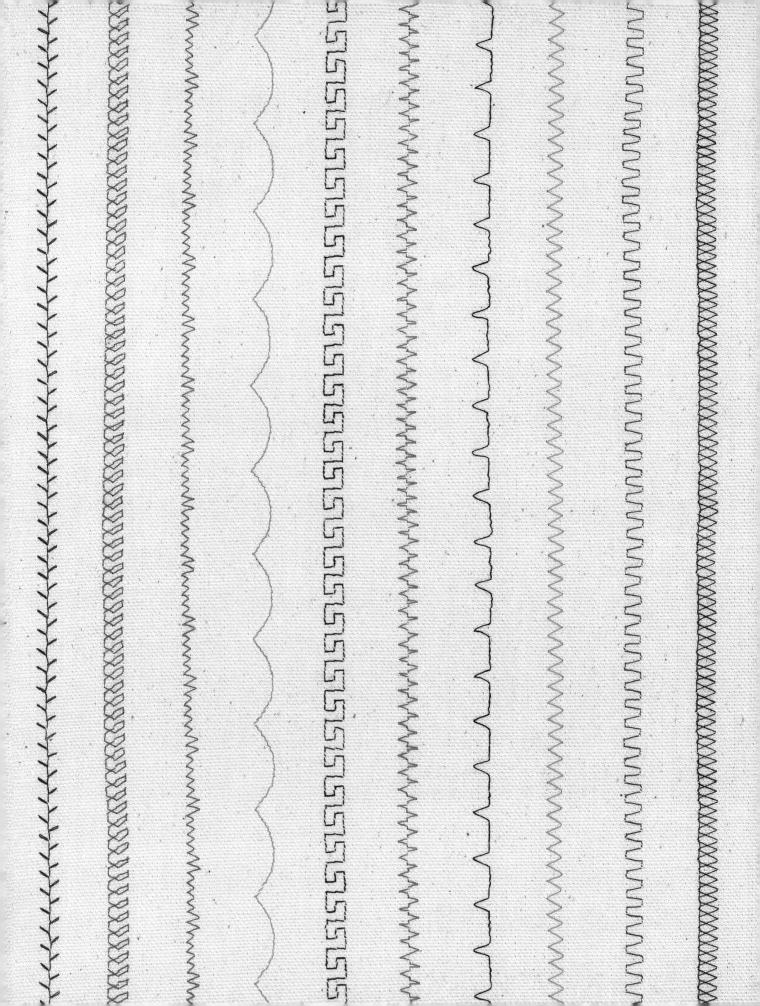